I0788387

LITTLE JOHNNY

WRITTEN BY
INGRID ULLRICH

ILLUSTRATED BY
RIGÓ ILLUSTRATION

LITTLE JOHNNY

Written by Ingrid Ullrich

TO MY NEPHEW, JOHNNY

*May your imagination always be as grand
and vibrant as you are.*

Once there was a little boy named Johnny,

Some days he was good, others, he was naughty.

He loved to dance, jump, shout, and play,

But sometimes Little Johnny got carried away.

He loved his superhero toys, and played with them
for hours,

Dressing up to look like them, pretending to have
their powers.

One day Mommy came to Little Johnny with some news,

"Pretty soon, you'll have a brother, and then there will be two!"

Little Johnny looked stunned as he dropped his head,

Hugging his toy to his chest, not one word to be said.

Johnny's father walked in, listening from the door,

"Son, what's wrong? What is the sad look for?"

"Mommy said we will soon have another boy,

But what about me and all of my toys?"

"Nothing bad will happen, your things will stay,

You'll be his big brother, and teach him to play."

"You will be his superhero, just like your doll,

Keeping him safe, protecting him from all!"

Jumping with glee, Little Johnny sprung to his feet,

Excited about his brother, who soon, he would meet.

Later that night, Little Johnny hopped into bed,

Closing his eyes after his story had been read.

Slipping into sweet dreams his baby brother was all
he could see,

Closing his eyes after his story had been read.

Slipping into sweet dreams his baby brother was all
he could see,

Growing side by side together, what best friends
they will be!

The end